Toby the Tram Engine

Based on *The Railway Series* by the Rev. W. Awdry
Illustrations by *Robin Davies and Jerry Smith*

EGMONT

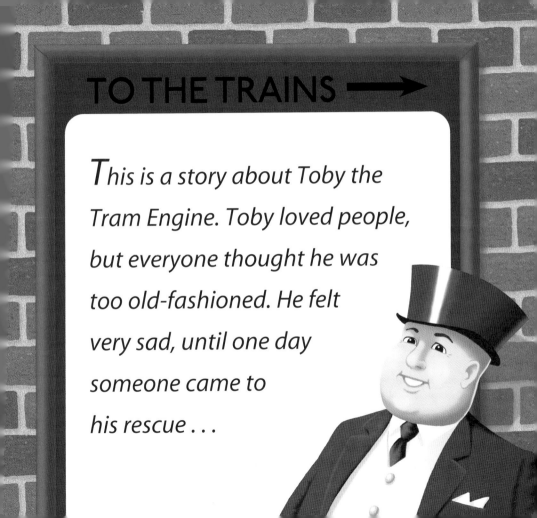

*T*his is a story about Toby the Tram Engine. Toby loved people, but everyone thought he was too old-fashioned. He felt very sad, until one day someone came to his rescue . . .

Toby was a Tram Engine. He had cow catchers and side plates, and a coach called Henrietta. Toby loved people and was always happy when he could help them out. He was such a cheerful engine that people liked to help him, too.

Toby and Henrietta worked on a little line near a holiday town. They worked very hard, taking trucks from the farms to the Main Line. But they had very few passengers.

"It's not fair!" grumbled Henrietta, one day. "The buses are always full of passengers, even though they often have accidents. We never have accidents, but I have hardly *any* passengers."

"I can't understand it," said Toby, feeling sad.

Sometimes the people on the buses laughed at Toby and called him old-fashioned. This made Toby cross.

One day, a car stopped nearby and two children jumped out.

"Come and look at this engine!" called the little boy.

A nice-looking stout gentleman followed them with two ladies.

"That's a Tram Engine," explained the stout gentleman. "It's a special kind of steam train."

"Can we have a ride in it?" asked the little girl.

They all climbed into Henrietta and the Guard blew his whistle. Toby set off, feeling proud to have passengers.

"Hip, hip, hurray!" sang Henrietta as she rattled along.

The stout gentleman and his family enjoyed their ride. "Thank you, Toby," they said.

"Peep! Peep!" whistled Toby in reply. "Come again soon!"

"We will!" called the family, and they waved goodbye.

As time passed, Toby and Henrietta had fewer and fewer trucks to take to the Main Line, and they had no passengers at all.

One morning, the Driver looked very sad.

"It's our last day, Toby," he said. "The Manager says we must close tomorrow."

At the end of the day Toby puffed slowly to his shed. "Nobody wants me," he said, unhappily.

But the next morning Toby had a big surprise! A letter had arrived for his Driver.

"It's from the stout gentleman," said the Driver. "Do you remember him, Toby?"

"I remember him very well," said Toby. "He knew how to speak to engines."

"No wonder," said his Driver. "That gentleman was The Fat Controller!"

The Fat Controller needed extra help on his Railway, and he had thought of the nice little engine he met on holiday. Toby could hardly believe it!

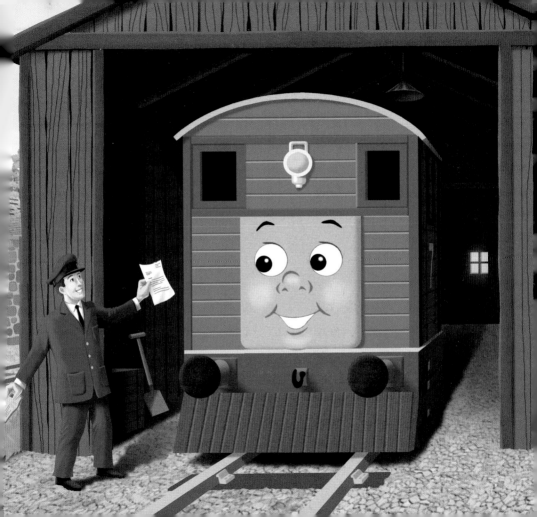

Toby and Henrietta set off that day. They were very excited. When they arrived at Tidmouth Sheds, The Fat Controller came to meet them.

"Thank you very much for asking me to come, Sir!" said Toby.

"I'm glad you're here, Toby!" said The Fat Controller. "I hope you will work hard and be a Useful Engine, just like Thomas."

"I'll try, Sir!" said Toby.

Thomas came up to say 'hello'. He showed Toby what to do and they were soon very good friends.

Toby loved working on The Fat Controller's Railway and he soon learned to be a Really Useful Engine.

Next to Thomas' branch line was a little cottage. The lady who lived there liked to see Toby and Thomas puffing past. She always waved to them from her window.

"That is Mrs Kyndley," Thomas told Toby. "She isn't very well, and she has to stay in bed all day."

"Poor lady," said Toby. "I wish we could help her." From then on, Toby and Thomas always whistled to Mrs Kyndley when they passed her cottage.

One day, it was raining hard as Thomas hurried along the track with Toby following behind. Suddenly, Thomas' Driver pointed at Mrs Kyndley's cottage.

"Something's wrong!" he said.

A big red cloth was waving out of the cottage window.

"Perhaps Mrs Kyndley needs help!" said Thomas' Fireman. Thomas stopped carefully, just before a bend in the track.

Thomas' Driver and Fireman hurried to the cottage. But when they looked around the bend in the track, they understood why Mrs Kyndley had stopped them.

"A landslide!" said the Driver. "Mrs Kyndley has saved our lives!"

Mrs Kyndley had seen the landslide, and had waved her red dressing gown out of the window, to warn the engines.

The line was cleared the next day, and a very special train puffed along the branch line towards Mrs Kyndley's cottage. First came Toby, then Thomas with Annie and Clarabel, and last of all came Henrietta. The Fat Controller was there, too. Everyone wanted to say 'thank you' to Mrs Kyndley.

When they reached the bend in the track they stopped. The people got out and climbed up to the cottage. Toby and Thomas wished they could go, too!

Thomas' Driver gave Mrs Kyndley a new dressing gown. The Guard gave her some grapes and Toby and Thomas sent some coal as a present.

"The engines and I would like to give you these tickets for a trip to the seaside," said The Fat Controller. "We hope you will get better in the sunshine!"

"You are very kind!" said Mrs Kyndley.

Toby and Thomas blew their whistles to say 'thank you'! Toby felt very happy that he had come to work on The Fat Controller's Railway. "Hip, hip, hurray!" sang Henrietta!

Thomas Story Library

Thomas

Edward

Henry

Gordon

James

Percy

Toby

Emily

Alfie

Annie and
Clarabel

'Arry and Bert

Arthur

Bertie

Bill and Ben

Peep!
Peep!

BoCo

Bulgy

Charlie

Cranky

Daisy

Dennis

Diesel

Donald and
Douglas

Duck

Duncan

The Fat Controller

Fergus

Freddie

George

Harold

Hector

Hiro

Jack

Jeremy

Kevin

Mighty Mac

Murdoch

Oliver

Peter Sam

Rocky

Rosie

Rusty

Salty

Sir Handel

Skarloey

Spencer

Stepney

Terence

Trevor

Troublesome Trucks

Victor